CREATURE CAMPERS

SURPRISE UNDER THE STARS

JOE McGEE

ILLUSTRATED BY BEA TORMO

Andrews McMeel
PUBLISHING®

SURPRISE UNDER THE STARS

Andrews McMeel Publishing
a division of Andrews McMeel Universal
1130 Walnut Street, Kansas City, Missouri 64106

www.andrewsmcmeel.com

Epic! Creations, Inc.
702 Marshall Street, Suite 280, Redwood City, California 94063

www.getepic.com

20 21 22 23 24 SDB 10 9 8 7 6 5 4 3 2 1

Paperback ISBN: 978-1-5248-5570-3
Hardback ISBN: 978-1-5248-5783-7

Library of Congress Control Number: 2019947822

Design by Ariana Abud and Wendy Gable

Made by:
King Yip (Dongguan) Printing & Packaging Factory Ltd.
Address and location of manufacturer:
Daning Administrative District, Humen Town
Dongguan Guangdong, China 523930
1st Printing – 12/16/19

Norm tossed and turned in his bunk. He rolled to the right, and his blanket fell off. He rolled to the left, and his sheets crumpled into a bunch. He stretched. His head hit the wall and his feet fell off the end of the bed.

Norm had no idea that any of this was happening. He was fast asleep and dreaming of a giant berry casserole.

But Norm was the only one asleep. It was the second night of camp, and not everyone at Camp Moonlight was as relaxed as the sleeping Bigfoot.

Oliver buried his head under his pillow. "I can't sleep," he moaned. "I keep thinking I hear something out there in the dark."

Wisp pushed his mop of hair up and out of his eyes. "Me too," he said. "It's so dark, it's scary."

"You don't think there's something out there, do you?" asked Oliver.

Something cracked outside their window.

"It's a monster!" Wisp shrieked.

"Norm!" Oliver shouted. "Wake UP!"

Norm bolted awake. He sat up so fast he bumped his head on Oliver's mattress. Oliver shot out of his bunk and flew across the room, where he landed in a tangled pile with Wisp and his blankets. Wisp and Oliver tumbled to the floor while Norm rubbed his head in a daze.

"Good morning, Creature Campers," said their camp counselor Zeena Morf, who was standing in their open cabin doorway.

"Whew," said Wisp. "Not a monster."

"But it's not—" began Oliver.

"Morning?" said Norm.

Hazel bounded into their cabin, thumping circles around them.

"It's morning, good morning!" she said. "Early morning. *Really* early morning. You should see the stars. Are you making a fort? Are you having a pillow fight? Pillow fights are fun!"

"We're not having a pillow fight," said Norm.

"Or building a fort," mumbled Wisp.

"It was so dark, I couldn't sleep," said Oliver. "I kept hearing things outside."

"I thought there were monsters," Wisp said.

Norm rubbed his eyes. "Noises? Monsters? I was dreaming of a delicious berry casserole."

"Funny that you should mention berry casserole," said Zeena, "because that's exactly what awaits you if you can

successfully complete your map and compass skills test."

Norm grinned. "Well then, what are we waiting for?"

Wisp and Oliver hit him with their pillows.

"Pillow fight!" yelled Hazel.

Zeena groaned and buried her face in her hands.

The stars were still bright in the sky when Zeena led the Creature Campers to the Camp Moonlight flagpole.

Furrow Grumplestick, the grumpy gnome who was their camp director, stood there waiting for them, clipboard in hand.

"Time's a-wastin', campers," said Grumplestick.

Zeena pushed the campers forward. "There was a—"

"Pillow fight!" said Hazel.

Grumplestick scribbled something on his clipboard. He did not seem amused.

"Today," he said, "you will learn basic map and compass skills."

"Map?" said Oliver. "Like a treasure map?"

"Well, that's *one* kind of map," said Grumplestick.

"Is the treasure buried?" asked Wisp.

"It's not buried," said Grumplestick. "Nothing is buried."

"So, there *is* a treasure?" asked Norm.

"Yes," said Zeena.

"No," said Grumplestick, at the same time.

"Yes? No? Which is it? Yes or no? No or yes? Is it treasure that's not buried? Or is it something buried that's not treasure?" asked Hazel.

"I told them about the berry casserole," Zeena whispered.

"I see," said Grumplestick. "Well, if you can successfully navigate your way to three checkpoints using the stars, a map, and a compass, you will not only get your Camp Moonlight map and compass skills certification, you will also get—"

"BERRY CASSEROLE!" shouted Norm.

"Berry casserole," said Grumplestick. "Along with an entire picnic spread."

Norm's stomach grumbled.

"The first step is to follow the North Star," said Grumplestick.

Zeena pointed to a star shining over their heads in the dark sky. "That," she said, "is the North Star."

Norm, Oliver, Wisp, and Hazel gazed at the bright white star. Norm was pretty sure that it was the same star that shone through his cave window back home.

"So," said Grumplestick, "follow the North Star until you reach the first checkpoint: a stone table. There you will find a map and the instructions for finding your way to the second checkpoint. At the second checkpoint, you will find a compass. Use the compass to guide you to the third and final checkpoint. Any questions?"

Norm raised his hand.

"Yes?" Grumplestick said.

"Will we be allowed to have seconds of that berry casserole?" Norm asked.

Zeena shook her head and sighed.

Grumplestick drew his eyebrows together and scribbled something on his clipboard.

"Begin," he said. "We'll be waiting at the last checkpoint with the picnic spread.

And if you don't arrive by noon, more berry casserole for us!"

He grinned through his beard.

As Grumplestick and Zeena walked away, Norm did not grin back.

"Seems easy enough," Norm said. "We just follow that bright star." He pointed to a star and started forward without waiting for anyone. After all, he thought, the sooner they got this done, the sooner they'd be eating berry casserole!

"Wait," said Oliver, staring up at the thousands of stars twinkling in the sky. "I thought it was *that* one." He pointed to the left of Norm's star.

"No way," said Wisp. "It's that star right there." He pointed to a completely different star.

Hazel pointed to one star after another. "Could be that one, or that one, or that one, or—"

"It's clearly the one I'm pointing at," Norm said, cutting her off. "It's definitely the brightest. That's the one that Zeena showed us. Besides, I'm the tallest, right? I have the best view. Now let's go."

Wisp crossed his arms. "Are you sure?"

"Would I risk losing berry casserole over this?" asked Norm.

"Good point," said Oliver. "But maybe we should try and get an even better look, to make sure."

Norm took a deep breath. "The more time we stand around here arguing over which star it is, the more time we waste. I don't know about all of you, but *I* am hungry."

"Well, gee, Norm," said Oliver, "if we go chasing after the wrong star, we're going to have a much bigger problem than hunger. We'll be lost!"

Norm thought for a moment. "Fine," he said. "I have an idea. If we all balance on top of one another, we'll be even taller. That way, we'll be able to see the sky better." Norm knelt down. "Oliver, climb onto my shoulders."

Oliver pulled himself up and onto Norm's shoulders.

"Hazel, you're next," said Norm.

"I'm not so sure about this," said Oliver.

Norm held his legs tightly. "Don't worry. I won't let you fall."

Hazel hopped up onto Oliver's shoulders.

"Okay, Wisp," said Norm. "You're going to get the best view of all."

Wisp took a big, long, deep breath and held it. He fluttered his wings as fast and hard as he could. Ever so slowly, he lifted off the ground and up to Oliver. He pushed harder and made it all the way up to Hazel.

"I . . . did . . . it," he gasped happily.

"Way to go!" Oliver said.

"Hold on to my antlers," said Hazel. "We're going up!"

Norm got to his feet with Oliver, Hazel, and Wisp carefully balanced on his shoulders. Together they were so tall that they could almost reach the top of the Camp Moonlight flagpole!

"All right," Norm said. "Wisp, can you see which star is the brightest?"

Wisp pushed his hair out of his eyes. He gazed at the sky.

"It's definitely that one," he said, pointing to a very bright star pulsing overhead.

But then the star moved. It had just been directly above them. Now it was moving across the sky in a slow line.

"It's moving away from us!" Oliver said.

"Quick!" Norm said, kneeling down again. "Everybody down. We've got to chase that North Star!"

Wisp scrambled off of Hazel. Hazel hopped down off of Oliver. And Oliver slipped off of Norm's shoulders.

Norm raced ahead. His long legs made for long strides, but no matter how fast he ran, no matter how long his strides were, he could not keep up with the star. "We're losing it!" he said. Finally, he had to stop to catch his breath.

It took a while for the other three campers to catch up with him. They found

Norm leaning against a tall pine tree.

"I'm not so sure the North Star is supposed to *move*," Oliver said.

"Is it supposed to be that close to the ground?" asked Wisp.

The star was moving faster and getting closer to the treetops, and it trailed a long, glowing line behind it.

The campers watched as the bright ball of fiery light crashed into the woods somewhere beyond them.

"Oh no!" Hazel cried.

"What?" asked Norm.

Hazel pointed to a pulsing glow. It cast a spooky light upon the trees and branches.

"Look," she whispered. "The sky has fallen."

MEANWHILE...

From inside the hollow trunk of a nearby tree, Barnaby Snoop, the world-famous carnival owner and creature collector, had watched the very same light fall from the sky. But that's not all he was watching.

Barnaby Snoop was spying on the Creature Campers huddled in the forest.

He grinned a sly grin. He rubbed his hands together.

"Why, that's no star," Barnaby said. "And it's certainly not the sky falling. That's nothing more than a meteorite. Meteorites contain a great deal of iron. Magnets attract iron."

Barnaby's grin grew even more sly. He had a plan to capture a new creature for his carnival— a Bigfoot named Norm! And his plan included one metal cage and a *very* powerful magnet.

EXCUSE ME! WOULD YOU MIND *NOT* SPOILING MY SURPRISE TRAP?

"If the sky has fallen, what's it doing still up there?" Wisp asked. He pointed to the canopy of stars above their heads.

It was no longer that dark. In fact, the sky had turned light grey—almost blue—as the sun began to rise. But the stars were still visible.

"Maybe it was just a *piece* of the sky," said Oliver.

"Or maybe it was a spaceship," said Hazel. "Maybe it was from outer space? Maybe they're Zeena's friends . . . or family . . . or friends *and* family. Ooh, ooh, I know: I'll bet it's a family reunion. A surprise family reunion. That's it!

We should tell Zeena. We should definitely tell Zeena. She'll be soooo excited."

"If it's a surprise, we definitely should *not* tell her," Wisp said.

Norm looked at the sky. He looked at the glowing woods. He didn't think it was the sky falling, or a *piece* of the sky falling, or a spaceship full of Zeena's family and friends who had arrived for a reunion. But he *did* think they should be worrying less about the weird light and more about finding their way to that berry casserole!

"Who cares what it is?" he said. "None of that helps us solve our problem, which is—"

"Which way is north?" Oliver finished.

"Exactly," said Norm. He sat down for a second and leaned his back against a thick pine stump. "We need to go north to find the map."

"That'll lead us to the compass," s aid Wisp. "And the compass will lead us—"

"Into my trap," chuckled Barnaby Snoop from the nearby hollow tree trunk. He quickly clamped his hand over his mouth.

"Did you say something?" Wisp asked.

Norm shook his head. "No, why?"

Wisp shrugged. "I thought I heard someone say something. Anyway . . . the compass will lead us north. Map. Compass. Grumplestick and Zeena."

"And berry casserole." Norm rubbed his back up and down the tree stump. It was covered with moss and felt quite nice. "This moss is super soft. I could fall asleep on this stuff."

"That's it!" said Oliver. "The moss! My parents are forest rangers. They taught me that moss grows mostly on the *north* sides of trees!"

Norm turned and looked at the stump. One side was heavily covered in moss. "Are you sure?"

Oliver straightened his shoulders and stood tall. "You can trust me. After all, I'm a forest-ranger-in-training!"

"So, if we follow the moss on the trees, we'll go north," said Norm.

"And get the map!" Wisp said.

Hazel bounded from tree to tree. "Here's some and here's some and here's some more!"

Norm, Oliver, and Wisp raced after
Hazel, following her deeper into the forest.
"Follow that jackalope!" Norm said.

MEANWHILE...

A very devious Barnaby Snoop was watching them and grinning. Soon, they would have their map. And then they would have their compass. And once they had their compass, the only thing left to do was use his magnet to trap them!

"Since the compass needle is attracted to magnetic north, I'll use my supermagnet to create an even stronger pull," he said. "And then, they'll follow my fake north right to me!"

Oliver had been right. By following the trail of moss, the campers soon found themselves in a small clearing. In the middle of the clearing was a large, flat, oval stone. It was carefully balanced on a smaller round stone.

"This must be the stone table that Grumplestick was talking about," said Norm.

"Look," said Wisp. "There's something on top of it."

Sure enough, a rolled-up map lay on top of the table. Norm carefully plucked it off the stone.

"Wheeeeeee!" Hazel said, thumping and scampering around the clearing. "We won! We won! We won!"

"Hazel?" said Wisp.

Hazel stopped leaping and bounding.

"Wisp?" she said.

"We still have to make it to two more checkpoints."

"Oh yeah," Hazel said. She leaned in to look at the map. "Whee," she whispered.

Norm unrolled the map, and a small note fell out and fluttered to the grass. Oliver picked it up.

It read:

CONGRATULATIONS, CREATURE CAMPERS. YOU HAVE COMPLETED THE FIRST PART OF THE QUEST. NOW FOLLOW THE MAP TO THE SECOND CHECKPOINT. HURRY UP! I'M GETTING AWFULLY HUNGRY, AND IT'S JUST ME AND ZEENA AND ALL THIS FOOD.
  - F. GRUMPLESTICK.

Norm spread the map out so everyone could see it. There was a purplish smudge on the paper that he thought looked awfully similar to the berries in berry casserole.

"No!" Norm shouted. "No, no, NO!"

"What?" Oliver asked. "What's the problem?"

"Don't you see it?" Norm asked. He jabbed his big finger at the map.

"The X?" Wisp asked.

The map showed the stone table, and there was also a great big X where the compass should be. In between, there were a whole bunch of footprints set out in anything *but* a straight line. Each different direction had a number to go along with it.

"No," Norm said. "That smudge. They're *already eating the berry casserole!*"

"We'd better hurry," said Hazel, "before it's all gone."

"Now you're making sense," said Norm.

"All we have to do is follow these dance moves," said Hazel, pointing to the footprints on the map.

"Those aren't dance moves," said Oliver. "They are the number of paces."

"But whose paces?" Norm asked.

"There's only one way to find out," said Wisp. "We'll start with the first set: Everyone walk thirty-three paces east and see where that takes you."

Norm, Oliver, Wisp, and Hazel all lined up at the stone table, facing north, and then turned to their right.

"Okay," said Norm. "We're facing east now. Thirty-three paces. Go."

"Wheeeeeeeeeeeeeee!" said Hazel, tearing off through the underbrush and disappearing into the forest.

Norm, Oliver, and Wisp all looked at one another.

"She'll be back," said Wisp.

Norm strode forward, counting his paces.

He reached twenty-seven and stopped when he came to the edge of a very tall waterfall. His strides were too long.

"That is a loooong way down," he said.

Wisp counted a full thirty-three paces, but he didn't make it out of the clearing. His strides were too short.

Oliver's thirty-three steps took him out of the clearing. When he stopped, he noticed a set of long footprints that looked like they could belong to Zeena.

"Hey guys!" said Oliver. "I think I'm on the trail!"

"Wheeeeeeeeeeee!" Hazel came tearing back. "I saw a moose and a deer and a squirrel and a crow and a bear. I think I saw a bear. I might have

seen a bear. It might have been a shadow, though. I was moving *very* fast."

"Hazel," said Oliver. "Let's just stick together."

Norm and Wisp joined Oliver and Hazel. Norm held up the map.

"Seventeen paces north," he said.

Oliver turned to his right. That was north. He counted off seventeen paces.

"Twenty paces east."

He turned right again and walked twenty paces east.

They continued this way through the woods, with Norm reading off directions and Oliver counting off paces. North, then south, then west, then south, then east, until finally they reached a small pond.

"This looks like the place," said Norm. He pointed at the pond on the map.

An old weeping willow tree sat at the edge of the pond, its branches dipping into the water. The water was green and covered with lily pads, and in the middle of the pond there was an old log. And on the old log there was a frog. A great big green bullfrog.

"Ribbit," said the frog, watching them from its spot on the log.

Tied to the back of the frog was the very thing the Creature Campers needed: a compass.

Getting the compass off the back of the bullfrog turned out to be very, *very* hard.

Norm reached out as far as he could, but even with his very long arms, he could not quite reach the frog.

The bullfrog sat on its log, watching him.

"Ribbit."

Oliver ran around to the other side of the pond. He made loud noises to try and startle the bullfrog into moving. But the noises didn't bother the bullfrog at all.

"Ribbit."

Wisp held his breath and squeezed his eyes shut and fluttered his wings as hard as he could. He lifted a few inches off the ground and fluttered over the pond, over the lily pads, and almost to the log. But when he opened his eyes to see how far he'd gone, he got very excited. He stopped holding his breath and yelled, "I'm doing it! I'm flying over the water!"

Unfortunately, the minute Wisp stopped holding his breath, he also stopped moving his wings. And the minute he stopped moving his wings, he stopped flying. He fell into the pond with a great big KERSPLUNK!

"Ribbit." The bullfrog leapt from the log onto Wisp's head, and then onto a lily pad.

Norm held on to the weeping willow's branches and leaned out as far as he could. His fingers were almost at the bullfrog when the branch broke.

Norm flailed his arms. He tried to catch himself. He reached for anything he could find, but there was nothing to grab but air. Norm landed heavily in the murky water with a gigantic SPLASH!

"Ribbit." The bullfrog leapt to the
marshy land at the edge of the pond.

"Gotcha!" said Oliver. He reached
down with both hands to grab the

bullfrog, but his feet got stuck in the mud and the bullfrog leapt up between his outstretched fingers. All Oliver grabbed was a big, wet handful of oozing mud.

"Ribbit, ribbit." The bullfrog hopped away from the pond with the compass still tied to its back.

Norm buried his giant head in his giant hands. "We're doomed! We'll never catch that frog. We'll never get the compass. We'll never get that berry casserole!"

"Hazel to the rescue!" Hazel said.

Hazel stood face to face with the bullfrog. Whatever it did, she did the opposite. When it hopped left, Hazel ran right. When it hopped right,

Hazel ran left. Left, right. Right, left. No matter how high or how far it hopped, Hazel was right there.

"Wheeeeee!" she said.

Finally, the bullfrog stopped jumping and croaked, "Riiiibbbit."

Hazel scooped it up. "Sorry to bother you, mister bullfrog," she said.

She untied the compass from its back. "Thank you, mister bullfrog," she said.

The bullfrog leapt from Hazel's hands onto Oliver's shoulder, then onto Norm's knee, then onto Wisp's head, and finally back onto its log.

"Ribbit."

"That was a fun game, guys, don't you think?" said Hazel.

Wisp, Oliver, and Norm did *not* think it had been fun. In fact, they thought it had been anything *but* fun.

"We don't have time for games," Norm grumbled. His stomach grumbled with him. "We need to go north, and we need—"

"Berry casserole," Wisp mumbled.

MEANWHILE...

Barnaby Snoop had just finished putting the final touches on his trap. It consisted of:

- ✓ One red-and-white checkered picnic blanket with a berry casserole in the middle of it
- ✓ One large metal cage hanging above the red-and-white checkered picnic blanket
- ✓ One GIGANTIC electromagnet

"And now," said Barnaby Snoop, watching the Creature Campers through his spyglass, "I'll simply wait for you to use your compass. When I want you to come my way, I'll just turn up the power on my magnet. *I* will

control where your compass points and mark my words—it will point right into my trap."

Barnaby's stomach growled. The berry casserole smelled very good.

Perhaps, he thought, I'll have just a little. One small piece. A sliver of berry casserole—nothing more than a bite.

There was a note on the back of the compass. Hazel read it while Norm, Oliver, and Wisp wiped the mud and pond gunk off of themselves.

"Blech, you guys stink," Hazel said. "Okay, all we have to do is use the compass to go one degree northeast."

"That's it?" asked Norm.

"That's it," said Hazel. "That's what this note says: *One degree northeast will bring you to our picnic feast.*"

"Well, what are we waiting for?" Oliver asked.

Norm's stomach rumbled. "Picnic feast," he groaned. "Berry casserole."

"We'd better hurry, or Grumplestick will eat it all!" said Wisp.

Hazel held the compass until the needle pointed north. "There's magnetic north," she said. "So we need to go . . . " She turned the compass until the needle rested on one degree. "This way."

Norm, Wisp, and Oliver followed Hazel as she bounced along, following the compass.

The sun was shining and the forest was alive with chattering chipmunks and scampering squirrels. It was almost noon!

"Hey guys," said Hazel. "Want to sing a song? A camp song? Who knows a good camp song? Maybe we—"

"No!" Norm, Wisp, and Oliver said, all at the same time.

"Geez," mumbled Hazel. "Fall in a pond and you become all grumpypants."

MEANWHILE...

What was intended to be only one slice of berry casserole, one *small* sliver, turned out to be the entire thing. Barnaby Snoop's buttons were ready to pop. He had purple berry stains in his mustache and beard. Suddenly he realized that he'd been so busy eating casserole that he'd forgotten to watch where the campers were going. He quickly raised his spyglass to one eye. He spotted them—but they were going the wrong way. They were headed away from him!

"That won't do," Barnaby said. He rushed to his giant electromagnet. He wrapped his fingers around the power lever.

"Just a little bit of power should do it,"
he said. He pulled the lever.

Hazel stopped moving. The compass
needle wobbled. It turned right, then left,
then right again.

"I think we have to go a little more
this way," said Hazel. She pointed toward
her right.

MEANWHILE...

Barnaby Snoop watched the campers move farther away from his trap.

"That can't be!" he said.

He turned up the power even more. This time the Creature Campers turned back in his direction. They took a few steps, stopped, and looked at their compass. Then they turned away again, going in the opposite direction.

"What is the meaning of this?!" Barnaby shouted.

Hazel tapped the compass. One minute, the needle was pointed to her right. The next minute, it spun in a complete circle and then pointed to her left. She kept trying to head one degree northeast, but she had to stop and adjust every few seconds. They were going in a zigzag through the woods.

"I think it's broken," she said.

"Maybe it got wet," said Oliver.

"Who would tie a compass to a bullfrog?" asked Wisp.

"Grumplestick," said Norm. "He's probably eating all of the berry casserole right now."

But Furrow Grumplestick was *not* eating all of the berry casserole. In fact, he was eating *none* of the berry casserole. Instead, he and Zeena Morf were enjoying a nice spread of cheeses and discussing the current value of leprechaun gold and whether or not unicorns could use their horns to roast hot dogs over a campfire.

MEANWHILE...

Barnaby Snoop saw what the problem was. The campers were getting closer to the meteorite that had fallen from the sky. The meteorite was a really strong magnet—so strong that it was interfering with *him* interfering with the campers' compass!

"There's a simple solution, Barnaby," he said to himself. "I'll just make my magnet more powerful than the meteorite."

And that's what he did.

Hazel watched the needle spin and spin and spin, until it finally pegged dead to her left. She held the compass in front of herself and hopped toward the place where Barnaby Snoop and his trap were waiting.

Oliver, Wisp, and Norm looked at each other and then followed Hazel.

While the boys continued to follow Hazel, Hazel followed the compass. And the compass followed the powerful pull of Barnaby Snoop's giant electromagnet.

The compass led them to a small clearing in the woods with nice, green grass. A single red-and-white checkered picnic blanket had been spread out. In the middle of the blanket sat a large, empty dish. The dish had a few small clumps of purple in it.

"We found it!" said Hazel. "I knew we could do it."

"But . . . but . . . " Norm's shoulders slumped. "We're too late!" he groaned. "Grumplestick ate all of the berry casserole!"

Suddenly, the compass shook and wiggled. It began to pull out of Hazel's grip. She held on as tight as she could, but she started to stumble forward. Something was pulling Hazel and the compass toward itself.

Oliver reached out and grabbed her,

but he was pulled forward, too. Norm grabbed Oliver, but whatever was pulling them was too strong. It began to drag Norm—who was holding Oliver, who was holding Hazel, who was holding the compass—forward.

Wisp grabbed Norm and flapped his little wings as fast as he could. It was just enough to stop them from moving forward.

Hazel gripped the compass.

Oliver held Hazel's antlers.

Norm held Oliver's belt.

And Wisp hugged Norm's leg as tightly as he could.

They couldn't let go and they couldn't move back. But at least they weren't being pulled forward any more.

MEANWHILE...

"Oh no you don't," said Barnaby Snoop. "Just a few more feet and you'll be directly under my cage. And then I just have to release the cage lever and WHAM! One Bigfoot for my carnival. I'll be rich. I'll be famous. I'll be rich *and* famous!"

He pushed the power up as high as it would go. Past the red line. Past the label that read, *Caution: Do NOT push power past the red line.*

He pushed it until he couldn't push it any farther.

The buttons tore loose from his coat.

The compass tore free from Hazel's hand.

The giant electromagnet hummed and shook.

A spoon flew past Norm. Then another. Then a fork. Then another spoon and fork. Then a pot, then a pan, and then several pots and pans.

A canoe hurtled over their heads. Norm, Oliver, Wisp, and Hazel dived to the ground.

Loose change. A watch. A bicycle. A door handle with the door still attached. A unicycle. A muffin pan.

It was a nonstop barrage of metal objects flying toward something just out of sight.

"Maybe the sky *is* falling," Norm said. He covered his friends with his long arms. "Don't worry, I'll protect you!"

"But what about the casserole?" Oliver asked. "There might be just a little bit left."

"I can always get more casserole," Norm said. "I can't always get friends like you three."

MEANWHILE...

Barnaby Snoop did his best to avoid the swarm of metal objects. The cage he had suspended and camouflaged above the picnic blanket strained and groaned and tilted toward the magnet.

"It's out of control!" he said, struggling to turn off the electromagnet. The power lever would not move. He tugged harder. It still would not budge. He planted both feet on the magnet and pulled as hard as he could.

The switch broke free in his hand. Barnaby Snoop staggered back. His hand whacked into the cage lever and he landed with a thud, on his behind, in the middle of the clearing.

The cage crashed to the ground, trapping him underneath it.

And somewhere, deeper in the woods, something bigger was being pulled his way.

"Hey, look!" said Oliver. "Isn't that the nice man from the lake?" He squinted. "Sure looks like him. He must be camping. But that's a strange tent to sleep in. Won't he get cold at night in a tent that has bars for walls?"

"Hey!" shouted Hazel. "Hey mister! Watch out! Watch out for that—"

BANG!

"Canoe," she finished, as the canoe banged into the cage and stuck there.

Norm cupped his hands and yelled, "Look out! There's a—"

CLANG!

"Unicycle," said Norm. The unicycle clanged against the cage and stuck.

"Here come some—"

BWONGGG!

"Pots and pans," said Wisp.

SPROINGGG!

"Hey, that's our *flagpole*!" said Hazel.

Then something rumbled. Something broke branches and flattened bushes. Something big and heavy and loud was crashing through the woods, picking up speed as it went.

"What—" said Norm.

"Is—" said Oliver.

"That—" said Wisp.

"SOUND?" shrieked Hazel.

They turned their heads to see what was making all of that noise.

A giant chunk of glowing space rock came rolling through the woods like a bowling ball. It hurtled right toward the campers.

"Look out!" said Norm. He wrapped Oliver, Wisp, and Hazel in his arms and leapt out of the way just as the meteorite rolled past them.

"Oh no!" Oliver said.

"The man from the lake!" Hazel pointed toward the cage.

"That giant rock is headed right for him!" Wisp shouted.

"Help!" Barnaby shouted. "Somebody help!"

Norm stood up. "Come on, Creature Campers," he said. "We have to save him."

Barnaby Snoop closed his eyes. He held his breath. He waited for the moment when the giant, rolling meteorite would slam into his trap—the very trap he was now trapped inside of.

But when he opened his eyes, he saw something completely unexpected: The creatures were trying to *help* him. They were trying to free him from the cage before the meteor crashed into it!

"Hazel, quick, get your antlers under the cage and pry it up enough for me to get my fingers under it!" Norm said. "Wisp, use your wings and lift with me. Oliver, get ready to pull Mister . . . "

"Uh . . . " Barnaby said the first thing that came to his mind. "Mustache! Mister Mustache, at your service."

Norm slid his fingers under the cage where Hazel had pried it up. "Your name is Mister Mustache?"

"That's me," Barnaby said.

"Mister Mustache!" Hazel said. "That's great. Get it? Mustache? Because you have a mustache?"

The meteorite grew louder and louder and rolled toward them faster and faster.

"Hurry!" Oliver shouted.

Norm heaved the cage up as high as he could. Wisp huffed and puffed and flapped his little wings as fast as he could. When the cage was lifted just far enough for Barnaby to slip out, Oliver grasped his hands and helped him scramble to freedom.

Barnaby Snoop and the Creature Campers hurried away from the cage as the meteorite hit it with an ear-splitting KA-GONG!

"That was entirely too close," said Oliver, brushing dirt and grass from his shorts.

"Mister Mustache, are you okay?" Wisp asked. "Mister Mustache?"

But Mister Mustache was nowhere to be seen.

"He disappeared," Hazel whispered. "Like magic."

However, Barnaby Snoop had *not* disappeared by magic. He had simply run away the minute the campers were distracted. One moment he'd been trying to capture them, and the next moment they'd been *saving* him.

orm clutched his rumbling stomach. "Oh well," he said. "At least we were able to save Mister Mustache."

"He must have been in an awful hurry to just leave like that," said Wisp.

"Magic," Hazel whispered.

"Glad he's okay," said Oliver.

"Me too," said Norm. "I just wish he would have shared some of his—"

Norm stopped. He sniffed the air. He sniffed left. He sniffed right.

"You guys smell that?" he asked.

Wisp kicked a tuft of grass. "It's not my fault I smell like a pond," he said.

"No." Norm took a step forward. A great big smile broke across his face. "It's berry casserole! And I'm sure it's this way!" He pointed back the way they'd come.

"Where there's berry casserole, there's a picnic," said Oliver. "And I sure have worked up an appetite."

"And where there's a picnic, there's Zeena and Director Grumplestick," added Wisp.

"And where there's Zeena and Director Grumplestick, there's our map and compass skills certification!" said Hazel.

"Hold on," Norm said. "I have to say something to you all."

"But Norm, the casserole," Wisp said.

"I know," said Norm. "But no matter how much I love berry casserole, I love you all even more. I'm sorry I acted so bossy and impatient." His stomach growled even louder. "My stomach is sorry, too," he said, laughing.

"Thanks, Norm," Oliver said.

"Don't worry about it," said Wisp. "Friends 'til the end."

"Water under the ridge," said Hazel.

"Bridge," Oliver corrected her. "Water under the bridge."

"That's what I said."

"No, you said 'ridge.'"

"What's that mean, anyway?" Wisp asked.

"Guys?" Norm said. "This way."

Norm's nose led the way. Before long, they crashed out of the woods and into a small field of soft grass and wildflowers. Zeena and Grumplestick sat on a red-and-white checkered picnic blanket. Between them was a giant basket of food—including the biggest berry casserole Norm had ever seen.

"Thought we were going to have to eat this all by ourselves," Grumplestick said.

"Fortunately, we made it." Norm gave Grumplestick a huge grin.

"Unfortunately, we don't have any utensils," Zeena said. She pointed back the way the campers had come from. "They all went flying that way."

Hazel bounded forward. "That's because the sky was falling and we thought it was the North Star, but it wasn't the North Star, and then we got lost but we followed the moss because moss always grows on the north side. That's what Oliver told us and Oliver was right because Oliver is smart and Oliver is a ranger-in-training and we found the map and did our paces. Well, not our paces. Oliver's paces. And we found the pond and the frog and

I caught the frog, but not before they all fell in the water. And the compass went left and right and left and right and there was that nice man from the lake having his own picnic and then everything was flying through the woods, including your utensils, and a weird metal tent fell over the man and Norm and Wisp lifted it up so he could escape and then he used magic to—"

Wisp clamped his hand over Hazel's mouth.

"Can we eat now?" Wisp asked.

Norm's stomach growled loudly.

Grumplestick smiled. "Yes. Help yourselves to some of Zeena's delicious homemade berry casserole."

Norm held up a knife and fork he'd scooped up back at the clearing where they'd saved Mister Mustache. "Allow me,"

he said, and he cut nice big pieces of berry casserole for everyone, serving himself last.

"Congratulations, Creature Campers," said Grumplestick. "You passed your map and compass skills test." He picked up his clipboard and scribbled noisily.

"Well done," said Zeena. She reached into another basket and handed each of them a small, glowing stone.

Norm placed his in his palm. It hovered just above his hand, pulsing with a soft blue light.

"Whoa," said Oliver. "What is it?"

"A small piece of space crystal," said Zeena. "From my home planet. The sky isn't falling. It's there, watching, twinkling down at you. And when you go to sleep tonight, these stones will shine for you like the moon. They'll help you see that there's nothing to be afraid of in the dark."

"We'll be sure to sleep better now!" said Wisp.

"We don't call it Camp Moonlight for nothing," said Grumplestick. "Now who wants some more berry casserole?"

Norm, of course, raised his hand.

MEANWHILE...

Barnaby Snoop marched back to his carnival tent. All this time he'd been trying to capture that Bigfoot, to put him in a cage, and then suddenly he, Barnaby Snoop, had been in a cage. And he had not liked it. Not one bit!

"Those creatures freed me," he said. "They saved me from that giant space rock. And from that lake creature!" Barnaby Snoop tugged on his mustache. "Maybe one good turn deserves another. Perhaps there's a way that I can repay them. After all, Barnaby Snoop is a man of integrity!"

He stood up, squared his shoulders, and looked at himself in the mirror.

"Barnaby, old chap," he said, "it's time you returned the favors those Creature Campers have done for you!"

ABOUT THE AUTHOR

Joe McGee teaches creative writing at Sierra Nevada College. An avid cartoonist, board game player, and role-playing gamer, Joe is also the author of the *Junior Monster Scouts* chapter book series and three picture books: *Peanut Butter & Brains*, *Peanut Butter & Aliens*, and *Peanut Butter & Santa Claus*. He lives in a quiet little river town with his wife (also a children's book author) and their puppy, Pepper.

ABOUT THE ILLUSTRATOR

Bea Tormo is a children's book illustrator by day and a comic artist by night. She lives near Barcelona, Spain, where she enjoys being part of a community of artists. Besides children's books, Bea works on comic books, magazines, webcomics, and fanzines. She especially loves drawing grumpy people and monsters.